This Book Belongs
To

_____

To order additional copies, please contact:

BookSurge Publishing, www.booksurge.com, 1.888.308.6235, orders@booksurge.com
or visit Amazon.com

To learn more about Brenda Hasse visit: www.BrendaHasseBooks.com

To see more of Alison Hatter's illustrations visit: www.hatterstudio.com

A Unicorn for my Birthday

History Of The Back Creek Rocking Horse Company

Nestled in the shadow of Poor Mountain, near Bent Mountain, Virginia, is a toy workshop that produces high quality, hand crafted rocking horses. They are modeled after the Chincoteague Island, Virginia and Corolla Light, North Carolina wild ponies. The designer and modern day Geppetto, Ed Kane, owns and operates the Back Creek Rocking Horse Company. His rocking horses, illustrated in this book, are sold and shipped worldwide.

The Back Creek Rocking Horse Company would like to thank the following people:

Sarah and Cindi, for their love, support, and devotion, and Bob Paust, for his beautiful trims and fringes.

To Dad, for all of the campfire stories.
B.H.

To my little Elias, with love.
A.H.

A Unicorn for my Birthday

Written by Brenda Hasse
Illustrated by Alison Hatter

It's my birthday today. I can hardly wait.
Everyone is coming to help celebrate.
We have cake with ice cream, balloons, and more,
family and friends bringing presents galore.

I have opened my gifts from everyone.
Such lovely presents. Oh boy! That was fun!

Wait just a minute. There's one more to go.
In Grandpa's arms is a gift with a bow.

He placed the last gift upon the floor.
Another present! Who could ask for more?
I rip open the paper perplexed as can be,
there are two blue eyes staring back at me.

With a mane and tail,
it looks like a horse.
But the point on its head
makes it different of course.

I circle the gift
in contemplation...

And look to Grandpa
for an explanation.

Grandpa placed me gently upon his knee.
Encircled in his arms, he began his story.
"This mysterious animal from long ago,
is called a unicorn, just so you know.

"It represents good luck, hope, and love
and is said to be a gift from above.
It is also a symbol of purity
with its mane, tail, and hair as white as can be.

"It's a magical creature with a mystical horn
that counteracts poison and cures the forlorn.

The unicorn makes its horn glow bright
when healing others or to create a night-light.

"It roamed wild and free and had great fun
frolicking and playing under the sun.
Valleys looked spotted with white polka dots
as large herds grazed in fields of forget-me-nots.

"Each spring baby unicorns are born.
They have a little bump for a horn.
As they grow older their horns become longer
and their magical powers grow stronger.

"The Queen of the unicorns rules to protect.
She is old and wise and has earned her respect.
For she has the longest horn as her crown,
it signifies her stature that is well renowned.

"The unicorn's powers became well known
with stories of healing and luck overblown.

"As always with humans, their greed increased and they began hunting the gentle beast.

"The unicorns were aware of the danger.
They took to the woods away from the stranger.
They hid in the forest where it is scary
and were warned of intruders by a kind fairy.

"Deep in the forest by sharing a feast,
fair maidens claimed to have tamed the shy beast.
Their picnics consisted of sweet cherry tarts,
tea, and currant scones in the shape of hearts.

"Within the safe forest dim and gray,
the unicorn lives to this very day.

Legends say they can be seen in the mist,
but there are some who doubt they truly exist."

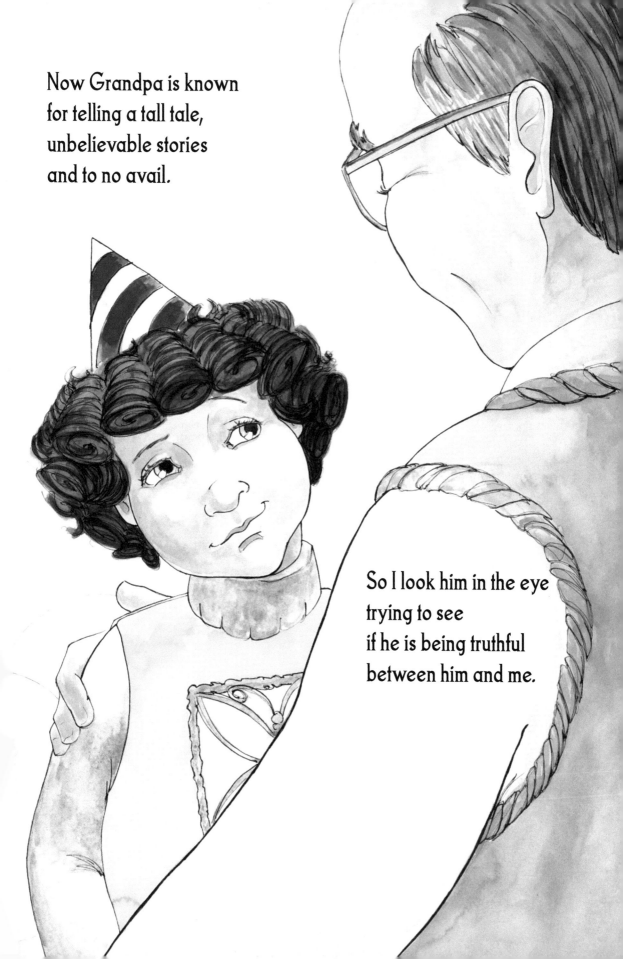

Now Grandpa is known
for telling a tall tale,
unbelievable stories
and to no avail.

So I look him in the eye
trying to see
if he is being truthful
between him and me.

There was a gleam in his eye as he spoke.
And I believed his story might be a joke.

"Are unicorns real?"
I asked, curious to know.
He replied,
"See for yourself,"
as he let me go.

I went to my gift
and touched its eye,
its horn, mane, and tail
and then gave a sigh.
"He feels real to me,"
I said climbing astride
to rock back and forth
on a mythical ride.

The End

CPSIA information can be obtained
at www.ICGtesting.com
Printed in the USA
LVHW07n0819100318
569384LV00019B/154/P